ROSCO THE RASCAL at the
ST. PATRICK'S DAY PARADE

Rosco the Rascal #4

By Shana Gorian

Illustrations by Ros Webb

Cover Art by Josh Addessi & Victoria March

For each petal on the shamrock
This brings a wish your way
Good health, good luck, and happiness
For today and every day.
~Irish Saying

CONTENTS

CHAPTER 1

BAD DOG, JACK

"Grrr..." the pint-sized Jack Russell terrier growled. "Ruff, ruff!"

Sparks, a polite young pug, wasn't sure why this disagreeable dog was barking at him, but he didn't like it. He hadn't done a thing to upset him. And he hadn't come all the way to the big city to march in the St. Patrick's Day Parade just to be hassled by a bad-tempered pup.

"Arf arf!" Sparks barked back. Sparks tugged on his leash—he wanted to get away from this irritating dog.

Second grader Mandy McKendrick held onto Sparks' leash tightly, trying to put some distance between Sparks and the unfriendly terrier.

"Ruff, ruff!" This time the little terrier lunged forward, sinking his sharp teeth into Sparks' ear.

"Oh my goodness!" cried Mandy as Sparks yelped in pain. She squatted down to place a protective hand over Sparks' head, glaring at the terrier's owner, who hadn't been paying attention to his dog. "Excuse me? Can you watch your dog, please? He just bit my dog's ear!"

Taking the terrier by the collar, the boy began to holler at the dog. "Not again! Bad dog, Jack!"

Mandy reached down to examine Sparks' ear, loosening her grip on his leash. The ear wasn't bleeding, but Sparks wasn't about to wait around for another attack. He tugged on his leash again. This time, it slipped from Mandy's hands. Sparks broke into a run, leash trailing behind.

"Wait! Sparks, come back here!" Mandy cried, chasing after him.

But Sparks was afraid, and he was quick! Although he was just a little dog, he scurried around long legs and under other leashes faster than Mandy could hope to do. In a few seconds, she had lost sight of him completely.

Oh no!

Now what?

Mandy wasn't too surprised that something had already gone wrong today. Things had not been going her way for the last several days. In fact, Mandy's luck had been downright bad all week. Still, she never thought for a second that it would be this bad—that she'd lose Sparks!

CHAPTER 2

JAMES, WE HAVE A PROBLEM

Sparks was the Bentons' pet pug. Mr. and Mrs. Benton, a retired couple who had moved in next door to the McKendricks, had generously allowed Sparks to join them for this special occasion, so that Mandy and James would each have a dog to walk in the parade.

The dressed up dogs were always a big favorite of the downtown St. Patrick's Day Parade crowd, and before the run-in with the nasty terrier, Mandy had been enjoying the festive atmosphere. People had smiled and waved at her, exclaiming at the adorable costumed dogs.

Mandy wore her green *Pinch Me, I'm Irish* T- shirt. Her long, brown hair was held back with a green ponytail holder, and a headband with sparkly green shamrocks clung to her head.

Mandy's ten-year-old brother, James, wore a green and white button-up shirt and a goofy top hat. A fifth-grader with red hair and freckles, James was about as Irish-looking as any American-born boy could be. He enjoyed watching the St. Patrick's Day Parade every year and thought it would be fun to march in it this year.

James held the leash of their large, friendly German shepherd, Rosco, and grinned at the attention from the crowd as he and Rosco walked the parade route.

Because of the large number of people and dogs in the parade, James and Mandy had become slightly separated from one another. Mandy slowed down to let Rosco and her brother catch up.

"Oh, my gosh! James, did you see what just happened?"

"No. What happened? Where's Sparks?"

"Uh, we have a problem—a big problem." Mandy explained the run-in with the terrier and Sparks' disappearance.

"Are you serious?" James's eyes grew wide as he slowed down to take in her news.

A few other dog-walkers quickly overtook them, so he picked up his pace again, rather than trip over a tangle of leashes.

"Yes, I'm serious. He's gone!" Mandy said. "He was really scared of that dog, and, I guess...I don't know—he just ran away! I went after him, but...well, I lost him!"

James looked up at the tall buildings and the crowds of people everywhere. "Oh, man. This is *not* good."

Mandy bit her lip. "I know! And this is *just my luck*. I knew something like this would happen. If only I would've just done the school project, then all this bad stuff might not have happened."

"Don't start *that* again. This has nothing to do with you refusing to make a leprechaun trap."

"You don't know that," Mandy said. "I've had *so* much bad luck since I decided not to make one. I'm sure the leprechauns jinxed me—it's been like this all week!"

"Well, who knows? Maybe. But you've got

to stop blaming all of this on that project."

"Alright, James. Fine," Mandy said. "But what are we going to do about Sparks? Can you just help me? We've got to start looking for him."

CHAPTER 3
THE LEPRECHAUN TRAP

Mandy was afraid something bad might happen today. Ever since she had decided *not* to make a leprechaun trap for school, bad luck seemed to be affecting everything in her life. It was like the leprechauns knew that she had turned her back on them and were out to get her.

First, it was only little things that went wrong—like when her pencil broke in half for no reason, and when she tore a hole in one of her new socks, and when she got in trouble because she forgot to feed Rosco one evening.

Then, bigger things started happening. Her dad's car got a flat tire when he drove home from work one night. She left all of her library books at home on school library day, so she couldn't check out any new books for two whole weeks. And then it rained on the day of her school picnic at the park this week, so the picnic had been canceled.

She was worried that the bad luck would get even worse. And now it seemed it had.

Even though Mom said these bad things weren't related to one another—that bad things just happened sometimes—Mandy was sure that the bad luck was all because she refused to make a leprechaun trap.

Every March the children had a bonus assignment—to make a leprechaun trap at home and bring it in the day before the holiday. To be fair, it *was* optional. She didn't *have* to make one.

A leprechaun trap was any kind of contraption that a student could dream up that would trick a leprechaun into climbing inside. Some students made traps that looked like top hats with ladders made of sticks. The little leprechauns could climb up and hop in.

Other traps resembled pirate treasure chests or magical looking fairy beds—with real moss, pebbles and sticks to remind them of their homes. The key was to offer a bit of treasure—perhaps some fake gold coins or chocolate candy—anything that would trick a leprechaun into climbing inside.

The teachers at school said the leprechauns would enter their classrooms on the night before St. Patrick's Day in search of treasure. The kids would have left out their traps that night, and the hope was that one of the leprechauns would try to steal some of the treasure and become trapped.

Because if he were trapped inside, the kids would actually be able to see—*see* a real leprechaun! They wouldn't have held him captive for more than a few minutes. No one wanted to hurt the little guy. The kids only wanted to see one in person, ask him a few questions—about magical things or gold, or maybe some riddles or legends, or where the end of the rainbow is—and then send him on his way, no harm done.

So every year Mandy's teachers would ask each of the kids to make a leprechaun trap and bring it into school the day before St. Patrick's Day. Then, all they had to do was wait for the leprechauns to sneak into their classrooms overnight.

But Mandy had been getting tired of the whole thing. Every single year since kindergarten, Mandy had built a trap, often staying up late with Mom the night before it was due, working hard to do her very best. Almost all the kids made one, in fact. But the problem was—no leprechauns ever became trapped.

Now she was in second grade, and she was sure it would be the same story all over again. The only thing the leprechauns ever did was leave a big mess all over the classroom—tiny, green footprints and overturned desks, piles of paper thrown about the room, green smudges on the windows. But there was never a leprechaun anywhere to be seen.

Sometimes they left treats, too. But the whole class shared those, so Mandy wouldn't miss out on treats just because she didn't make a trap. Nevertheless, no one ever seemed to catch one.

So Mandy wasn't going to do it, not this time. She wasn't about to pour her heart and soul into her work and wish as hard as she could to see a leprechaun, just to be disappointed again. She would skip it this year. She was done with it.

But ever since she had made that decision, the bad luck had started. St. Patrick's Day was Monday. Today was Saturday—Saturday at the parade.

Yesterday, when the leprechaun traps were due at school, another bad thing had happened. Mandy's best friend Trisha had gotten sick. Trisha had left school early, right before lunch, because she threw up. And now, Sparks—that sweet little pug that Mandy was supposed to look after—was missing.

M-I-S-S-I-N-G!

Everywhere Mandy went it seemed like a black cloud was following her around. It seemed like the leprechauns thought that she didn't believe in their magical powers, and now, she, herself, seemed to be trapped in an endless string of bad luck. The worst thing was: she had no idea how to make it end.

CHAPTER 4
DOGS ON PARADE

A parade was something completely new to Rosco. Decked out in a shiny, new green bow tie, Rosco had been enjoying the attention of the parade-goers. He wagged his tail, tongue out, enjoying himself and grinning—until now. Now, he perked up his ears, listening closely to James and Mandy. He could hardly believe what he heard.

His best little buddy and next-door neighbor, Sparks, was missing? Here, in this crowd of thousands, that charming little fellow was all by himself? He might get lost, or trampled, or stolen! No, this was not good.

Rosco glanced around, hoping he could spot his pal. Maybe this was all just a mistake. Maybe Sparks, with his cheerful little smile, was somewhere nearby.

But it wouldn't be easy to spot him, since all of the dogs in the parade were dressed up for the holiday.

There were dogs dressed as leprechauns in tiny top hats and topcoats, with fake orange beards! Other dogs wore green capes or bandanas around their necks. Still others wore strings of beads or shamrock sunglasses. It was a sight to see!

There were dogs wearing green feather boas around their necks, long orange braids made of yarn, or pretty green barrettes clipped to the fur around their ears. Some sported silly green tutus around their waists.

Rosco could tell that some of the dogs weren't too happy about the costumes, although others seemed to love wearing them. *At least Sparks and I only have to wear hats and ties,* Rosco thought.

Yes, Rosco had probably seen over a hundred dogs this morning, including some Irish setters and even some Irish wolfhounds. But he'd seen a few *dozen* dressed up pugs. Sparks would definitely be hard to spot in this crowd.

"James, what are we going to do?" Mandy

repeated.

"I don't know, Mandy. I really don't know," her brother said, agitated. He looked around, scanning the crowd as they walked, growing more worried by the minute. "Mandy, I really can't believe this! How could you let go of the leash?"

Mandy blinked—tears began to well up in her eyes. "It was an accident, James. I didn't mean to! I'm sorry! Okay?"

"I know! Okay. Don't cry. We're going to find him. Let's just try and think straight. Are you sure he ran ahead of you, not that way, toward the sidewalk?" said James, pointing.

Mandy wiped her eyes, sniffling. "I'm sure. He ran straight ahead through all those dogs and dog walkers."

"Okay. Well, at least we know which direction he went. But we'll never catch up to him if we keep marching in the parade. We have to get out of here. Come on." He turned and headed for the edge of the street.

Rosco and Mandy hurried along, quickly

side-stepping in front of other dogs and leashes. Soon, the three of them squeezed through the tight crowd and found an empty spot on the sidewalk. They stopped to get their bearings.

"Okay, so where do you think he would go?" James said.

"I don't know. He could be anywhere," Mandy said. "Anywhere he'd be safe from that horrible Jack."

"Well, that narrows it down," James said, once again overwhelmed. "This is going to be impossible!"

"No, it's not, James!" Mandy said. We just need to start moving and keep on the lookout. We have to find him. He couldn't have gotten that far."

"Okay. Yeah, I guess you're right," said James, taking a deep breath. "Okay, let's get moving." He looked around at the happy faces watching the parade. "Maybe we'll get lucky. You know, with the Luck of the Irish? It's got to be here, everywhere!"

Mandy frowned. "Not with me around."

"Oh yeah," said James. "I almost forgot."

CHAPTER 5
BAGPIPES AND KILTS

The parade looped for about one mile through the city, among skyscrapers and along busy avenues. The city was an hour's drive from the McKendrick's house and although they'd been downtown before, the kids weren't too familiar with the area. So Mr. and Mrs. McKendrick had told the kids to walk the entire parade route as instructed, stay with the dog walker group, and meet them at the end when the parade was over. Only one person could accompany each dog in the parade, so their parents weren't able to march with them. The parade organizers had assured the McKendricks that all the dog-walker kids did things this way.

"Hey, maybe Rosco will be able to sniff him out," Mandy said, trying to stay positive. "Rosco, can you smell Sparks anywhere...?"

Just then, a clamor of loud music approached, drowning out the rest of her sentence. A Celtic marching band—dozens of men dressed in plaid kilts, overcoats, and plaid knee socks—pounded their drums and blared their bagpipes, marching in steady formation down the street. James recognized an upbeat version of one of his Grandma's favorite songs: *When Irish Eyes Are Smiling*. He knew it well because his grandfather sang it often. "Those Irish eyes make *me* smile, little lass!" Grandpa would say, faking a thick Irish brogue.

Next, row after row of Irish step dancers—young girls in colorful, richly decorated dresses—followed the marching band, kicking up their knees and tapping their toes in time to the lively music, arms straight at their sides. James and Mandy stopped to gaze at the girls' amazing footwork.

But Rosco tugged at his leash.

"What's the matter, boy?" James said. "We can't go losing you, too. Stay with us."

But Rosco couldn't listen. The bagpipe music was hurting his ears. He tugged at his leash again.

"Rrrr!" Rosco whined. He shook his head back and forth—his bow tie was itching now, too. He wanted to run. The noise was almost too much to bear. He tugged again and barked.

"We've got to get away from the music,

James!" Mandy shouted, pointing to her own ears. "Rosco can't take it. It's too loud! Come on!"

"Oh, okay!" said James, glancing at Rosco in surprise. "Let's go!"

The three of them started quickly down the sidewalk once more, whisking around mothers pushing strollers, dads holding kids on shoulders, and folks perching on tippy toes to see over the people in front of them. James and Mandy saw people in silly orange wigs, or oversized green sunglasses, or sparkly green top hats in every direction.

But soon, Rosco and the kids were far ahead of the band and dancers, and the noise level returned to normal.

"Are you okay, Rosco?" Mandy said, slowing to catch her breath. Rosco's tongue dropped out, panting, and his grin returned.

"He looks okay now," James said, running a hand down Rosco's back.

Rosco was indeed feeling better. His ears were still ringing, but at least they didn't hurt anymore.

"Okay, good," Mandy said. "Sorry about that noise, boy."

As they moved forward again, Rosco pressed his nose against the sidewalk, looking for even a trace of Sparks' scent.

"Look! Rosco is trying to sniff him out!" Mandy said.

But Rosco quickly moved on. *Nope, nothing here,* he thought.

"But I wonder if maybe Sparks is hiding somewhere? Maybe the music hurt his ears, too?" James said, and began scanning a nearby alley between two tall buildings as they passed it.

"Or what if someone grabbed his leash and took him to Lost and Found?" Mandy asked.

"I doubt they have even a Lost and Found," James said.

"Oh," Mandy said, frowning again. "Yeah, of course they wouldn't. Because if they did have a Lost and Found, we would've found him by now, and that would mean I was having *good* luck. But we all know that's not the way it is. My luck is anything but good right now."

James rolled his eyes. "Well, I guess we're going to have to find Sparks without luck, then. Anyway, maybe all of those bad things were just a coincidence, Mandy?"

"They can't all be a coincidence, James. I've never had so much bad luck in my life. I just wonder when it's going to stop. Or how?"

"Listen, let's not get sidetracked about your luck right now," James said, stepping over a crack in the sidewalk as they walked. "We have to find Sparks before the parade is over, and we don't' have much time." James looked at his watch. "Otherwise, Mom and Dad will never let us do this kind of thing by ourselves again."

"I know. I know, James! Mom and Dad will be so mad," Mandy answered. "But I'm even more worried about Mr. and Mrs. Benton. What will they say when they find out we lost their poor little dog in the big city? They'll be so upset! Sparks will never be able to come over and play with Rosco again."

Rosco lifted his head, alarmed at this news.

"*If* we find him, that is," James said. "And what do you mean—we? You lost him. I didn't."

Mandy pouted. "I know, James! I already apologized. It was *my* bad luck that did this! I didn't *mean* to lose him!" She walked faster. "What's gotten into you today, anyway?"

Rosco continued listening. *Ah-oh. This is not good,* he thought. *Here they go again.*

"I'll tell you what's gotten into me, if you really want to know. I've been waiting patiently for three weeks to be in this parade—I've never done something like this before. It was so cool—people cheering and waving to us, treating us like celebrities! And Rosco got to hang out with all those awesome dogs back there. We might've even gotten on the TV news! But just like that—we were done!" He snapped his fingers. "Twenty minutes into the parade and bam—we were out! All because of you!"

Mandy stared hard, first at James, then at the ground, slowing her pace. Her eyes began filling with tears again. She stopped walking. "You're right, James. It *was* my fault. I'm probably jinxed forever."

CHAPTER 6
THREE WISHES

Come on, guys, get back on track, Rosco thought, resting his gaze on Mandy and then on James. *Sparks needs us.* But both kids remained quiet, their backs to one another.

Maybe I can snap them out of this, Rosco thought, nudging his nose against James' hand. James glanced down at Rosco, who let his tongue drop out and started to pant. The doggie smile usually worked.

James gazed for a moment at the big, dopey grin on his dog's adorable face. He sighed heavily and turned to look at his sister.

"Aw man. I'm sorry, Mandy. It's not that big of a deal. I can always walk Rosco in the parade next year. We probably wouldn't have gotten on TV anyway. Let's just get back to finding Sparks."

Mandy took a deep breath and rubbed her eyes. "It's okay. I'm sorry I ruined the day for you, James. I didn't mean to lose him."

She reached out a hand to pet Rosco's head as they picked up their walk. Rosco's soft ears were very soothing when she was all worked up. The kids fell in step with each other again, with Rosco in between.

"You *will* get rid of your bad luck, somehow, Mandy. I'm sure you will." James sighed and cleared his throat. "Okay, so it looks like we have about an hour and a half until we see Mom and Dad, since they told us to meet them at noon," he said. "Let's try and find Sparks by then."

Mandy sniffled. "James, do you think there's any way I can talk to the leprechauns, so I can ask them to lift this jinx they put on me?" Mandy asked.

"Well, you can always try to capture one. You know, like, with a trap. Then he'd be forced to talk to you," said James.

"What? What are you talking about?" said Mandy. "Hey, if you're just making a joke, it's not funny. I asked you a serious question."

"I'm not making a joke," James said. "Don't you know the legend? I thought one of your teachers would've told your class why people make leprechaun traps in the first place."

Mandy's eyes widened. "No, they haven't told us anything—what legend? I have no idea what you're talking about!"

"Seriously? Miss Fitzgerald told our class. Then again, she's Irish and knows all this cool stuff, so maybe that's why she told us. I can't believe all this time you were complaining about your luck that you didn't know this!" James looked at Mandy, raising his eyebrows.

"Well, what is it? Go ahead—tell me!" Mandy cried, picking up her step.

"Okay, so according to Irish folklore, leprechauns are tiny people who spend a lot of their time hard at work making shoes. They store all of the coins they earn in a pot of gold, hidden at the end of the rainbow."

Mandy listened closely. "Okay, that makes sense."

"Legend has it," James continued, "that if a leprechaun is ever captured by a human, he has the magical powers to grant the person three wishes in exchange for his release."

"You're kidding me? I never heard that!" Mandy said.

"That's why I thought you weren't thinking straight when you refused to make one this year. Because every time you build a trap, you get the chance to make three wishes come true!" said James.

"Oh my goodness! If I had known all of that, I definitely would've made a trap! I wonder why my teachers never told us?" Mandy paused. "Maybe they want us to make traps every year just for the fun of it?" she said. "Or maybe because it's like an art project, and it's good for us."

"Or maybe your teachers never mentioned it because they didn't want you guys getting too worked up," James said. "Some of the kids in your class would probably make crazy wishes, like for all of the desks to turn into candy or something."

"True," said Mandy. "Good point. Anyway, there's still time to make a trap before it's too late! I could make one at home tomorrow and leave it out overnight, because Monday is St. Patrick's Day. Maybe I could trap a leprechaun and then he could grant me my wishes? He could take away this bad luck!" Mandy said. "Finally!"

"That's the best idea I've heard all day," said James. "Especially if it makes you stop complaining about your luck." He laughed. "Whew, I wish I had told you that story earlier!"

"Me too!" said Mandy. "Meee too!" More thoughts began to swirl around in Mandy's head. "But James, do you know if that legend is true? I mean—this can only work if everything you say is true."

"I don't know, Mandy. It *is* just a legend. But sometimes, certain things about legends can be true. And you'll never know unless you try."

CHAPTER 7
KNEE SOCKS

As this new idea settled in, Mandy began to feel much better. *Maybe I can fix my luck,* she thought.

Soon she, James and Rosco reached another section of the parade. Miniature, old-fashioned yellow cars raced back and forth across the street, driven by older gentlemen in round black hats with gold tassels. The men seemed to be performing an elaborate comedy routine, nearly running into one another, zipping back and forth, tooting their horns, and hollering funny but harmless insults at one another.

The kids stopped to watch. "It's the Shriners—Dad's favorite part of the parade! They're so funny!" Mandy said. "I wonder if Mom and Dad saw them yet?"

James laughed at the tiny cars zipping down the street. "Probably not, since Mom and Dad are watching the parade from where it ends. Anyway, Sparks won't be out there," he said. "He's smart enough to stay out of traffic. Come on! Let's go!"

They followed the sidewalk again, dodging the crowd, and soon came upon another spectacle. Eight beautiful brown horses marched in two rows of four. Police officers in uniform rode the horses. One of the riders carried an Irish flag on a flagpole, proudly displaying its colors of green, orange and white. Another held tall an American flag.

"They call that the mounted unit, Mandy," James told his sister proudly. "They're the police unit that patrols on horseback. Mike told me that once—you know—because his dad's a policeman."

"Neat!" Mandy said, watching the eight horses clip-clop down the street in perfect formation. "And look! They're wearing socks!" The tall horses were indeed dressed in matching green socks that covered their legs from above the hooves to below the knees.

Eight times four is thirty-two, Mandy thought. "That means there are thirty-two knee socks right there! That's a lot of knee socks!"

"I didn't know you knew your eights already—that's really good for second grade," James said.

"Thanks!" said Mandy.

"Let's keep moving," said James. Rosco and Mandy dropped their gaze from the horses and followed.

Ahead of the mounted unit, such crowds filled the area that Rosco and the kids could no longer see the action very well from the sidewalk.

"What's up there?" Mandy shouted. "I can't tell!" She pointed at the street. It was getting very loud again.

"I can't tell, either!" James said. "Let's go see! But keep an eye out for Sparks. He's got to be out here somewhere."

James pulled Rosco's leash a little shorter

so it wouldn't become entwined around any parade-goers' legs.

CHAPTER 8
SEND IN
THE CLOWNS

Squeezing among dozens of tightly crammed tourists and city residents on the sidewalk, James, Mandy and Rosco finally reached the edge of the street. There, throngs of children held out their hands, catching the candy and beads that were being flung to the crowd. Rosco wagged his tail in excitement.

"It's the clowns!" Mandy exclaimed. She raised herself on tiptoes to see.

One clown rode a unicycle, balancing on the tiny seat perched over its one big wheel, as he juggled bowling pins in the air. Another

raced by in oversized shoes, riding a scooter.

The round nose and red smile on his painted white face made small children stop and stare.

Another clown rambled by in striped socks on tall stilts. Still others twirled Hula-Hoops or strutted by in rainbow tutus.

James scanned the street, hoping to spot the little pug somewhere— anywhere. He was starting to think they'd never find poor Sparks. He glanced at his watch. It was already 11:00am—only an hour left until they had to meet their parents. And this was the most packed the sidewalk had been, yet.

"Mandy, it's too crowded. We're never going to find Sparks here. We can't even see five feet in front of us. We should keep moving. Come on."

"This is because of my bad luck again, James. I know it," said Mandy.

"Oh, Mandy..." said James. "We already made a plan to try and fix your luck. Can't you stop worrying about it?"

Just then, a tired-looking clown in a fluffy orange wig stopped in front of them to tie some green balloons into the shape of a shamrock. The clown handed it to a very small boy standing next to Mandy, who ran off shouting with joy. Several more eager children raced over to claim the next balloon shamrocks.

"Me first!" they cried, pushing and shoving to form a line. One girl reached into one of the two large buckets dangling from the clown's wrist. She shuffled around in the bucket for a treat as the clown twisted and tied another balloon.

"Now hold on there, youngster," said the clown, trying to disguise his irritation. "Could you wait until I hand it to you, please?"

The tiny girl held up the piece of candy, stuck out her tongue at the clown, and bolted toward the sidewalk. Mandy's eyes grew wide at the girl's bad behavior.

"Well, I never..." said the clown, looking shocked. "Kids these days..."

"James, I have an idea," Mandy said.

Quickly, she reached down and swiped up three strands of shiny, green beads that had been thrown on the sidewalk.

"What are you doing, Mandy?"

"Let's give these clowns a hand. We can stay on the street and get past this huge crowd on the sidewalk if we do. After all, we *were* in the parade. Why not get *back* in it? You didn't' want to get out, after all. And it'll be faster, at least for now. Plus, it looks like they could use some help."

James opened his mouth to protest, but before he could speak, Mandy stepped up to the frazzled clown. "Hello, sir," she said, holding up the green beads. "Can we give you a hand with this stuff?"

"I don't see why not. I could use a few more hands," the clown said." Then, glancing at Rosco, he added, "I guess I could use a few more paws, too. Have at it, kids...and dog." He handed Mandy the bucket of beads and James the bucket of candy and grabbed another skinny balloon from his shirt pocket. "I'll get back to making shamrocks and wiener dogs now. Gee whiz, you'd think these kids never saw a balloon animal before."

James sighed, but a small smile rose from the corner of his mouth. "Alright, Mandy. I guess this could work."

Soon Mandy and James were tossing goodies to the kids on the sidewalk as Rosco trotted along. He wagged his tail, grinning, appreciating the attention he was getting from so many children. But he also made sure to sniff around for Sparks.

Nope, still no sign of him.

A clown's helper drove around in a golf cart, refilling James' and Mandy's buckets three times. Soon, Rosco and the kids had moved beyond the overcrowded area, buckets empty again.

"Let's get back to looking for Sparks now!" James called.

"Okay! I'm tired out anyway!" said Mandy.

The kids returned the buckets to their clown friend, who had finally caught up on making balloon shamrocks and now wore a genuine, relaxed grin. "Thanks, kids! And thanks, pooch!" he hollered.

CHAPTER 9
BANISH THE SNAKES

"Gosh, that was a lot of work, but it sure was fun!"

"Yeah! And at least we were *in* the parade again. But we should probably get back on the sidewalk now," James suggested.

Mandy chewed on her lip, thinking hard. The worry was beginning to return as the excitement of their last adventure wore off.

"Mom and Dad will be expecting us soon. Do you think we'll *ever* find Sparks?

"I was just wondering the same thing, Mandy. But he has to be here somewhere," James said. "He has to."

"I sure hope he's okay. I wonder if he's scared—or hurt?" Mandy said.

"Ruff, ruff!" Rosco barked.

"What's up, Rosco?" said James. "Did you pick up Sparks' scent?"

"Ruff, ruff!" Rosco barked again, facing the direction in which the parade was moving. James and Mandy looked ahead, trying to figure out what was getting Rosco worked up.

"I see some floats up there. Do you think he's barking at those?" Mandy asked.

"Only one way to find out," said James.

Rosco pulled at his leash, eager to move.

"Let's *follow* Rosco this time," James said, easing up on the leash. "It seems like he knows something we don't."

As Rosco led them down the sidewalk, Mandy and James heard festive music coming from one of the floats on the street. A large, flatbed truck held a band of musicians tapping their feet as they played their instruments—a flute, a fiddle, and a banjo. On the next float, men wearing tweed caps on their heads sang traditional Irish tunes as dancers performed a jig.

Next came a man on a float dressed in long green and gold robes and a bishop's hat. He had a long, white beard and carried a wooden staff in one hand and a wooden shamrock in the other. Rosco and the kids stopped to watch.

"Look, he's supposed to be St. Patrick— the patron saint of Ireland," said Mandy. "What's that legend about him again, the one about the snakes?"

"St. Patrick is said to have banished all the snakes from Ireland," said James. "They say he chased them all into the sea."

"You sure do know a lot about legends, James," Mandy said, lowering her voice. "Do you think this one's true?"

"Probably not," said James. "Miss Fitzgerald said there were never snakes in Ireland to begin with. After the last ice age ended, when the glaciers melted away, it was still too cold for snakes. And since Ireland is an island, they couldn't get there by land. So yeah, it's probably not true. There were no snakes to banish. Still, it's a neat story."

"Hmmm," Mandy said, scratching her chin. "I can't wait to be in Miss Fitzgerald's class," said Mandy, turning to see what might be coming down the street next. "Hey, look at that—a giant green bubble!"

A man walking backwards down the street held carefully onto a large bubble wand as a large bubble trailed along.

"Wow! That bubble must be four feet wide and eight feet long!" said James. "I wonder how he does that?"

"With an awful lot of soap—green soap!" said Mandy. James laughed.

"I thought for sure that Rosco picked up Sparks' scent back there. But he stopped pulling on the leash," said Mandy. "I wonder if he lost it."

"And it's almost twelve o'clock. Mom and Dad will be expecting us—like, *soon*," said James. "I saw the other dog-walkers pass us a while back, so they'll be reaching the end of the parade route pretty soon. Mom and Dad will be looking for us in that group."

"Oh, this is getting bad, James—really bad," said Mandy.

"I know, Mandy. But don't start getting all worked up again. Sparks has got to be around here somewhere." James looked down at Rosco, hoping for a sign—any sort of sign that Rosco might know where Sparks could be.

CHAPTER 10
THE RAINBOW FLOAT

Although he'd been enjoying the floats and street performers with the kids, Rosco was on high alert for his best little buddy. Something familiar had caught his attention a few minutes ago, and now he searched for it again, sniffing at the air. *Something's up,* he thought. *I smell something.*

"Top of the morning to ye!" A man with an orange beard shouted to the crowd.

"Look! There's a leprechaun coming this way!" Mandy cried, distracted once again.

The leprechaun man was dressed in green suit pants, a green topcoat and vest, and a rounded top hat. He wore a lime green bow tie, and on the black belt around his waist, a gold buckle shimmered.

"And look, there's a rainbow!" said Mandy. Rosco and James turned their gaze to an elaborately decorated trailer.

The moss-covered trailer was being pulled by a large pickup truck. On the trailer stood a huge arch, made of wood and painted in bright colors. It looked just like a real rainbow. Oversized artificial flowers, butterflies, rocks and mushrooms sat upon the moss. A lovely, little, thatched-roof cottage rested beneath the rainbow. Each end of the rainbow sat buried inside a giant pot of gold.

"Wow! That's so neat!" Mandy said. "That's not real gold, is it?"

"No chance," James said.

"Do you think that's a real leprechaun?"

"No chance of that either, Mandy. He's too big. Leprechauns are tiny. That's just a

man dressed up like one. He's probably a mascot for the float."

Rosco sniffed at the ground again, searching the sidewalk for another trace of the familiar scent.

The leprechaun mascot sauntered by, waving and tipping his hat, shaking hands with the crowd every so often.

"James, I have an idea. I wonder if this mascot could tell us if the legend about the three wishes is true?"

Here she goes again, James thought, sighing. "Okay. I guess it's worth a try, Mandy. Anything to set you straight."

CHAPTER 11
A TALL ORDER

"Excuse me, sir! Excuse me, sir?" Mandy called to the leprechaun man from the side of the street. "May I ask you a question?"

The leprechaun man strolled over and stuck out a hand. "Nice to meet ye, young lass," he said in a strong Irish brogue, smiling to the crowd of onlookers. "The name's O'Donnell. Whatever can I do you for?"

"Uh, pardon me?" Mandy said politely.

"I think he means—what did you want to ask him?" said James. A small crowd listened and smiled as the man chatted with Mandy and James.

"Oh—very nice to meet you, Mr. O'Donnell," said Mandy. "Well, sir, I wondered if you could tell me—sorry to keep you from your float—but I wondered if you could tell me—uh, is it true that leprechauns have the magical power to grant three wishes to someone who traps them, in order to be set free? My brother told me about the old Irish legend, and he thinks it might be true, but we aren't sure."

"Aye! That old legend's been around for donkey's years!" said Mr. O'Donnell. "But, lassie, your brother, here, is a wise, young lad. Because, as a matter of fact, it *is* true! It's as true as the day is long!"

Mandy looked puzzled again.

"That means it's true," James whispered.

"Oh, wow! Really?" Mandy said. "Well, that's great news, Mr. O'Donnell!"

"Really? Wow!" said James. He was as surprised as his sister.

"Now, I've got questions for you," said Mr. O'Donnell, leaning in toward Mandy, "why *ever* would ye want to know? And why is that such great news—are ye planning on trapping one 'yerself, miss?"

"Well, yes, if I can! See, I decided not to make a leprechaun trap for school," Mandy said. "That probably made the leprechauns mad, since they want us to leave them

58

treasure. So I think they jinxed me with bad luck. So now, I thought that if I make one at home and leave it out tomorrow night, that I might be able to trap one. And then he would have to grant me my wishes so I'd let him go free," she explained.

"Aye, that's a tall order, little miss!" he said.

The group of parade-goers listening to the discussion nodded and laughed.

Mr. O'Donnell went on. "May I ask you, lass—if ye were to trap one, what wishes would ye need him to grant ya? Is something wrong that needs fixin'?"

"Well, yes, Mr. O'Donnell. Actually, we lost our other dog here today at the parade." She reached out a hand to pet Rosco's back as she spoke. "His name is Sparks, and he's such a *little* pug. He ran away from me...it all happened so fast," Mandy's voice trailed off.

"Hours ago," James added. "And we can't find him anywhere. We're very worried about him."

"And it's all because I insulted the leprechauns, and they jinxed me," Mandy repeated.

"Oh, I see. I see. That is some fierce trouble you've got there. So, you're saying your first wish is to find 'yer little hound?" he asked.

Rosco listened quietly, afraid to interrupt this mysterious, yet charming, older gentleman. The rainbow float was almost out of view now, and Rosco wanted to catch up to it again, but whatever Mandy was learning from Mr. O'Donnell sounded important, and he didn't want her to miss it.

"Yes, my first wish would be to find Sparks—safe and sound," Mandy said.

"And, just to be clear, what would be 'yer second wish for the leprechauns, lass?" he asked.

"My second wish would be to take away this bad luck and bring back my good luck," Mandy answered.

"Aye, that's a good one. Those mischief-making leprechauns sure do know how to make ye miserable at times!" he said, chuckling. "You don't want to go upsetting the wee folk—nor insulting them, neither!"

Mr. O'Donnell smiled once more and looked back to Mandy. "I must be on me way soon, lass, so what would be 'yer third wish, if you were to trap 'yerself a wee leprechaun?"

"I only need two wishes, sir," said Mandy.

"But according to the legend, you get three wishes, lass!" said Mr. O'Donnell.

"But I only need two. I wouldn't want to take more than I need," said Mandy. "I just want to fix my luck. I wouldn't want to be greedy."

At this, Mr. O'Donnell and the others in the crowd who'd been listening smiled warmly, moved by Mandy's humble words.

"Aye, bonny lass, ye needn't capture a leprechaun tomorrow night, because you've already gone and captured me heart today!" The small crowd nodded in agreement. "I'll see what I can do, nevertheless—maybe they'll listen to me!" He smiled and waved to Mandy and James and the crowd.

"Thank you, sir! And thank you for telling me the truth about the legend!"

"Aye! 'Yer welcome! Now take care, lass! Take care, lad! Off ye go! I'm gunna head on!" Finally, he smiled at Rosco and waved to the crowd again, moving ahead toward the rainbow float.

CHAPTER 12
TRUST THE HOUND

As Mr. O'Donnell left to catch up to his float, Rosco wagged his tail. It was time to get a move on. The rainbow float was out of view. He let out a bark.

"What's up, Rosco?" James said. Rosco barked again. "I think we should let him lead the way again, Mandy."

"If you say so," Mandy said. "But I'm beginning to wonder if Rosco only smells food and is trying to lead us to it. If he's as hungry as I am, then he might just be leading us to the nearest corned beef and cabbage stand. A sandwich sure sounds good right now." Mandy's stomach growled.

James grinned. "That's always a

possibility. And it *is* almost lunchtime."

Rosco felt James loosen his grip on the leash. He was glad to have control again. But he wasn't concerned with food at the moment. He forged ahead, pulling James along. Mandy did her best to keep up.

They passed a sandwich stand, but Rosco didn't even pause. Winding through more crowds on the sidewalk, Rosco pulled them along until they'd once again caught up to the rainbow float.

"He brought us right back to Mr. O'Donnell's float! Rosco must've really liked him!" Mandy said. "James, something seemed unusual about that man, didn't it? I can't figure out exactly what..."

"I agree—but, wait!" James cried. He pointed to the rainbow float. "Look at what's facing the other side of the street!"

Perched atop one of the fake, giant, red-and-white-speckled mushrooms on the far side of the float, sat a little dog. It sported a green top hat and a sparkly green collar with a bow tie. Its coat was blond; its tail was curly. A leash draped from its collar. No one held the leash.

"Oh my gosh—could it be?" Mandy cried. "Could it be Sparks?"

"I think it could be!" said James. "It sure looks like him from here! But I can't tell for sure. He's too far away." He squinted and stood on tiptoe.

Rosco barked—he *was* sure. He knew that was his best little buddy, high up on that float, safe and sound. He thought he had picked up Sparks' scent the first time they saw the float. Then, they'd almost lost him.

But Rosco could smell him again. And now he could even see him!

He pranced around, beside himself with excitement. *Hooray—it's Sparks, at last! And the kids understand—they'll realize it's him! But wait—Sparks doesn't see us, and that float's still moving. I have to get him back before we lose him again!*

"What should we do, James? How are we

going to find out if it's him? Maybe we can get over to the other side of the street," Mandy said, glancing around.

Rosco yanked at his leash again, pulling with all his might. *Sorry kids, but I've got to take care of this!* he thought. *There's no time to waste! I'll be right back!*

James wasn't expecting such a pull and the leash broke free from his hand. "Rosco, wait!" he called, cupping his hands to his mouth. "Come back! Come back!"

But Rosco didn't. He scrambled into the street, straight past the performers, straight toward the rainbow float.

"Ah-oh," said Mandy. "He's going to see if that's Sparks, isn't he?"

"I'm thinking 'yes'," said James, stunned.

CHAPTER 13
A STROKE OF LUCK

Unsure what to do, James and Mandy watched with dread as Rosco approached the float and determined the easiest way to get up onto it.

"Oh no," said James.

"Oh boy," said Mandy. "Is Rosco going to get in trouble? Do you think someone's going to stop him? Maybe we should go grab him."

"Uh..." said James, looking around nervously as Rosco leaped up onto the parade float. "Um?"

"Aye, it's the big hound belonging to the bonny young lass!" Mr. O'Donnell called, having caught up to his position in the parade lineup. "Whatever could he be doing on me float?" he said, laughing. The crowd and Mr. O'Donnell watched as Rosco pranced across the mossy green bedding of the float, his shiny green bow tie still on his collar. They watched him stand up on his hind legs, and lean in to greet his friend, resting his front paws on the red-and-white mushroom. Sparks yipped with excitement at the unexpected sight of his best pal, and he, too, pranced about, thrilled as could be.

"It *is* Sparks, James! It's him!" Mandy cried. "Rosco found him!"

"Why, it looks like 'yer big dog found 'yer little dog, lass!" shouted Mr. O'Donnell. "That's right lucky, I'd say! Maybe the leprechauns are already goin' easy on ye?"

James finally let out a long breath, relieved that no one was shouting at his dog, or at him.

"Yes, Mr. O'Donnell! I'd say it's very lucky!" Mandy said, laughing, wondering if he was right. Then to James, she said, "Looks like Sparks found himself a comfortable ride.

No wonder we couldn't find him on the sidewalk or anywhere else! He was smart enough to get away from all the other dogs!"

James nodded. "No kidding!"

They watched as Sparks, panting and grinning, climbed down off the mushroom and hopped off the float with Rosco.

"I can't believe this!" said Mandy. "How could we have missed him the first time we saw that float?"

"I guess, because he was facing the other way, and he was kind of hidden by that big rainbow," James said. "Plus, we were so busy talking about the leprechauns, we almost missed this stroke of good luck! Thank goodness Rosco followed his nose!"

Mandy reached down to pick up Sparks as he and Rosco trotted up. Hugging the pug tightly, she kissed his little green top hat and sighed with relief. "Oh Sparks, where have you been all this time? Right here? I hope so! You had us so worried! Don't you ever go running off like that again, you sweet, little boy! I'm so glad to have you back!"

"And Rosco, what a good boy you are! You knew exactly where to find your buddy, didn't you?" said James. "What would we do without you, Rosco?"

Mandy turned to James. "You know, I thought there was something unusual about Mr. O'Donnell before. But now I'm sure of it! Maybe he has magical powers like the leprechauns? Maybe he already sent a message to the leprechauns and they already erased my jinx? Maybe that's why we found Sparks right after we talked to him. Do you think so?"

"You never know, sis. You never know!" said James. "This sure does make me wonder, though. Now, let's go find Mom and Dad and tell them about this crazy day before they think *we're* lost. Plus, I'm starving!"

CHAPTER 14
THE **CLUE HUNT**

Even though Mandy thought that maybe Mr. O'Donnell was responsible for Sparks' return and would do his best to speak to the leprechauns about her jinx, she wasn't taking any chances. If there were wishes to be granted, Mandy still wanted to capture a leprechaun so she might be able to fix her luck by herself.

When Monday morning arrived, Mandy hopped out of bed early to check on her trap.

She'd worked all day yesterday, carefully building a trap. She wanted it to look like an upside down top hat with a ladder leading up to a platform. On the platform, she had glued a handful of gold-wrapped chocolate coins and even a sign to catch the leprechaun's attention.

Mandy flipped the switch on her bedroom wall. The sun was not yet up and the room needed an overhead light if she were to get a good look at the trap. Kneeling, she peered down at it. But much to her dismay, no tiny man dressed in green was trapped inside. None of the coins was missing, either. She sighed heavily. But then her eyebrows shot up. *Wait, what's this?*

A small, folded up piece of paper sat in the trap. *Well that's odd,* she thought. *Where did this come from? And what is it?*

She picked up the note, unfolded it carefully, and began to read.

> *My dear lass, you see*
> *It's time for a game.*
> *You may not have trapped me*
> *Nor learned of my name.*

But you showed me a thing
more precious than gold.
Go ahead; play along
before the new day grows old.

To see what I mean
you'll search for some clues.
But you don't have to play.
It's your choice to choose.

More precious than gold? thought Mandy. *What in the world...?* She continued reading.

> *So if you'll join in,*
> *go find the first clue.*
> *Now off with ye, lass!*
> *Go look in your shoe.*

My shoe? Mandy thought. *Wow, what is this? It's so neat! I wonder what shoe he means?*

Mandy stood and walked over to her bedroom closet. There, on the floor, sat five pairs of shoes piled in a heap. Bending down, she lifted up one of the brown boots. Nothing unusual was there. She tried a pink sneaker with gray stripes, and inside of it was another very small, folded-up piece of paper.

"Oh my gosh! It's a clue!" she shouted. Grabbing it, she opened it carefully so as not to tear it. This one had only one verse.

Now onto the next one.
It's under a table.
You'll locate the clue
if only you're able.

If only I'm able? Hmm. Under a table? There were plenty of tables in the house. *Which table?* Mandy raced out of her bedroom and down the stairs. In the kitchen, her mother stood at the stove holding a spatula over a frying pan. The room smelled of maple syrup and scrambled eggs.

"Good morning, Mandy! You're up early. Guess what? I made you a special treat— green pancakes! Happy St. Patrick's Day, sweetie!"

"Yum! Thanks Mom," Mandy said, stopping to catch her breath. "It smells so good! But I can't eat breakfast yet—I'm on a clue hunt!"

"A clue hunt?" said Mom. "You are?" "What are you talking about?

"My trap didn't work, but a leprechaun

left me these clues, instead!" She held up the notes. "And there must be more, because it says there's one hiding under a table. I've got to find the right table."

Mom looked surprised.

Mandy knelt down and looked underneath the kitchen table. There, on the floor, was another note. "It's here!" Mandy could hardly contain her excitement.

This next clue, you'll find
if you check behind a door.
It's traveled far and wide
but I'll tell you no more.

Just then Rosco trotted into the kitchen and over to Mandy, his claws tip-tapping on the hard floor. He sniffed at the notes in her hands.

"A door—which door?" Mandy said. "Rosco, can you help me find the right door?"

Rosco's ears perked up and he gave Mandy a confused look. But he shuffled over to her side. He'd be glad to help her find the right door.

So Rosco and Mandy searched doors all over the house. At long last, they found another note behind the door in the coat closet.

"That makes sense, Rosco! Our coats travel far and wide with us every time we wear them out of the house!"

Mandy grabbed the new note and read it to Rosco.

> *Where might be your last note?*
> *Be it here? Be it there?*
> *Now off with ye, lass!*
> *Go look under a chair!*

"Under a chair? Come on, Rosco—I know just where to start!" Mandy raced once more to the kitchen, but no kitchen chair held a note. She tried the dining room chairs, but again, came up short. She tried the chair at Dad's computer and found nothing. Finally, she tried the living room. *Let's see, a sofa, a coffee table, and two big chairs.* "Maybe it's in here, Rosco?"

Bending down, she reached underneath one of the chairs. "I found it!"

She opened the note and glanced at Rosco. "This one's longer!" she said.

> *Dear Mandy,*
> *Although we did jinx you*
> *with terrible luck,*
> *your actions were humble,*
> *and the wee folk were struck.*
>
> *Not struck with a hammer*
> *nor struck with a nail,*
> *but with fondness, for you*
> *and your poor lost-dog tale.*
>
> *So the wee folk took pity,*
> *sent good luck your way.*
> *Now, listen, dear child,*
> *this St. Patrick's Day...*

Your wishes I have granted,
though trapped me, you did not.
Your small hound is back.
Good luck have you got.

So do heed these folktales,
these legends and lore.
For the magic is out there,
but I'll say no more.

Just trust that good things
will forever, you find,
just as long as you live
as both humble and kind.

"Wow!" Mandy returned her gaze to Rosco, speechless. Rosco stared back at her, wondering what this was all about. Several seconds passed. Finally, Mandy spoke. "This sure sounds important, Rosco. I *think* I know what it means. But I'm not sure I understand *all* of it. Let's go ask James and Mom to read it. Maybe they can explain."

"Mandy, these pancakes are going to get cold if you don't come and eat soon!" Mom called. "And it's almost time to get ready for school!"

"Coming, mom!" Mandy answered. She ran to the kitchen. James was there, devouring his breakfast. "You won't believe this!" She held up the notes to show them. "Now, the leprechaun left me a riddle!"

"A riddle?" said James, pausing before he dipped his next forkful of pancakes into a puddle of maple syrup. "Can I see those? Where did you get them?"

Mandy handed the notes to her brother and sat down at her plate. She explained how she'd found the first note in the trap and how it had led her from one clue to the next, and finally, to this longer poem. James looked astonished, just as Mom had, earlier.

He read the poem out loud while Mandy ate her pancakes. "Wow, that's really cool, Mandy! But I'm not sure it's actually a riddle. It sounds more like the leprechaun is trying to tell you something, not make you guess at something."

"I think he's right, Mandy," said Mom.

"Oh—okay. But it's written like a riddle. What I mean is that it's a little hard to understand. So, what do you think it means?"

"It's written so that the phrases are sort of backwards in some lines, kind of like Old English Verse," said James. "But the meaning isn't too hard to figure out if you reverse some words. Like here, 'though trapped me, you did not.' That just means you didn't trap him."

"Oh. Well, that makes sense," said Mandy. James examined the long note again.

"It sounds like the leprechaun is admitting that he did take your luck, but then he's saying why he gave it back, even though you didn't trap him."

Mandy listened carefully.

"I think what he's trying to say is that because you were so nice at the parade— helping people out, like that clown, for instance, and treating everyone around you so well, like Mr. O'Donnell...and being so concerned about Sparks and Mr. and Mrs. Benton, even though it was hard to have hope that we'd find Sparks...and then being humble and asking for no more than you needed—I think he's saying that you don't deserve the bad luck the leprechauns jinxed you with. So he decided to restore your good luck after all."

"Oh! I thought it was something like that," Mandy said, thinking hard. "That's pretty amazing.

Mom nodded.

"But what's this about legends and lore?" said Mandy.

James read the verse about legends again. "I think that it means you should take the leprechauns more seriously from now on. Don't ignore traditions like making a trap and offering them treasure every year. I guess they like to be offered treasure even if they don't always take it. And see this, where it says 'heed these folktales'?" James continued. "That means he wants you to believe in the legends."

"Very good, James," said Mom. "I'm impressed with your command of the English language!"

"Thanks, Mom," said James.

"But what do you think he's talking about, here? What's more precious than gold?" Mandy asked, then continued. "Do you think he means that I'll have good luck forever, as long as I'm humble and kind? Because good luck forever could be more precious than gold."

James glanced at the note again. "Yep, could be."

"Wow!" Mandy said. "I never have to worry about losing my good luck again!"

Just then a soft yip came from the porch. Sparks stuck his head through Rosco's doggie door and hurdled into the kitchen. Rosco rose from his spot on the floor and trotted over to greet him.

"Good morning, Sparks!" said Mandy. "Happy St. Patrick's Day, little buddy!"

James reached out to pet Sparks as the dogs sat down next to the table.

"Well, what a great start to a holiday, kids!" said Mom. "Now, you two had better go and get dressed. You have fifteen minutes until the school bus comes. And don't forget to wear green today!"

"We won't!" Mandy called, dropping her plate in the sink and heading for the stairs. James did the same and hurried off.

As Mandy boarded the school bus and took her seat, she waved goodbye to Rosco and Sparks, who watched from the front porch of the McKendrick's house. Both dogs wore their sparkly green bows again today, as they warmed themselves in the morning sunshine.

Mandy thought about her weekend, and wondered if Rosco had found Sparks just by using his nose, or if it was pure luck after all? She thought about all of the wonderful things she saw and interesting people she met. She was excited to see if the leprechauns had made a mess of her classroom today, *and* curious to see if anyone had managed to trap one. Secretly, she thought it was unlikely, especially now that she knew how smart and magical they were.

Then her mind wandered back to the poem and the parade. She realized that fixing her luck took hard work, believing in herself, and never giving up hope. It didn't matter whether or not a leprechaun put a silly jinx on her—she always had the power to fix things by herself. And that was kind of like finding the pot of gold at the end of the rainbow.

Quick Reference Vocabulary:

Aye: yes

Bonny: pretty

Brogue: [brohg] an Irish accent spoken in English

Celtic: [kel-tik] influenced by Irish, Scottish, Gaelic, or Welsh languages or traditions

Contraption: a device or gadget

Donkey's years: an expression used in Irish slang meaning 'a very, very long time'

Folklore: traditional beliefs, legends and customs of a people

Irish Jig: a form of traditional, lively folk dance and the accompanying tune

Jinx: a trick or spell

Lad: boy

Lass: girl

Mascot: an animal, person, or thing used as a representative symbol

Ramble: to walk aimlessly

Spectacle: anything presented to be seen; something impressive; also, eyeglasses

Sported: wore

The Author

Shana Gorian, originally from western Pennsylvania, lives in Southern California with her husband and two children, and the real *Rosco*, their German shepherd. She is Irish-American, herself, and loves to make leprechaun traps and attend St. Patrick's Day parades. Shana is especially good at making an Irish dinner of corned beef and cabbage.

The Illustrators

Ros Webb is an artist based in Ireland. She has produced a multitude of work for books, digital books and websites. Samples of her art can be seen on Facebook at: facebook.com/TheChildrensBookIllustrator/

Josh Addessi is a quirky illustrator and animation professor based in Northwest Indiana. He has digitally painted all manner of book covers, stage backdrops and trading cards. Samples of his art can be seen at http://joshaddessi.blogspot.com/

Victoria March is an illustrator and 3D sculptor. She aided in painting this book cover. Samples of her art can be seen at https://www.artstation.com/artist/victoriamarch

Note: Leprechauns are mythical elves from Irish folklore who are said to enjoy making mischief and hiding treasure. But they don't actually jinx people. They wouldn't mind if someone decided not to make a leprechaun trap. This is simply a story of fiction, written just for fun, and should not be taken as fact!

Rosco the Rascal

The *real* Rosco is every bit as loveable and rascally as the fictional Rosco, but he usually doesn't like to wear sparkly bow ties and hats. He loves to play with other dogs, though, and take walks in the city.

Fun Facts about Rosco:

Birthday: Earth Day, April 22

Favorite game: Rosco likes to play fetch but he doesn't always like to give back the stick or ball

Favorite time of day: dinnertime; and, also when the kids come home from school

Favorite toy: a rope toy, for playing tug-of-war and fetch

Favorite holiday: Christmas

Favorite pastimes: napping; chewing on chew toys; chomping on ice cubes; barking at coyotes in the evening

Favorite thing to do on a walk: sniff for traces of other dogs

Visit **shanagorian.com** to sign up for her email list so you'll know when she releases a new Rosco book. And be sure to join Rosco for more adventures, in these books!

A Wee Bit of Irish Wisdom

May you live a long life,

Full of gladness and health.

With pockets full of gold,

As the least of your wealth.

May the dreams you hold dearest,

Be those which come true.

May the kindness you spread,

Keep returning to you.

~Irish Blessing

Life is like a cup of tea;

it's all in how you make it.

~Irish Proverb

May the best day of your past be the

worst day of your future.

~Irish Saying

Made in the USA
Middletown, DE
30 January 2022

60013038R00061